Thomas, James and the Red Balloon

Based on *The Railway Series*
by The Rev. W. Awdry

EGMONT

It was summer holiday time on the Island of Sodor. But not for the engines. For them it was the busiest time of the year. They worked hard carrying holidaymakers around the Island.

One day The Fat Controller sent Thomas to pick up something very special from Brendam Docks.

"What have you got there?" said Percy.

"A balloon," replied Thomas.

"A party balloon?" asked Percy excitedly.

"No," said Thomas. "This is a very special balloon." He chuffed away, leaving Percy feeling very curious indeed.

Thomas hurried along and soon arrived at an
airfield. Hot air was pumped into the balloon.
There was a big basket underneath and people
were climbing into it. James arrived with
some coaches.
"What is that?" asked James.
"It's a hot air balloon," explained Thomas.
"Holidaymakers can ride in it!"

Then, as if by magic, the hot air balloon rose silently up into the sky. The engines could see the people inside looking over the edge of the basket.

"What if it takes our passengers away?" huffed James. "What would happen to us then?"

"I hadn't thought of that!" replied Thomas. James chuffed away, and Thomas felt very worried.

The passengers on the platform looked up in the sky, as the red balloon floated above them and out of the station.

"What a beautiful balloon," they all said.

Everyone wanted a ride in the red balloon.

The balloon could be seen by everyone on the Island of Sodor. Donald gazed at it for so long, he nearly ran into some parked trucks.

"It's a floating basket with people in it!" exclaimed Donald.

"Whatever will they dream up next?" said Douglas.

James and Thomas were waiting at a level crossing for Bertie to cross the line. Thomas was still worrying about the balloon.

"It does look nice," said Thomas. "But what if it takes all our passengers?"

"Passengers belong on trains!" said James crossly. "Not in silly balloons!"

Then something big and round and red drifted straight towards them.

"We're out of hot air!" cried a voice.

Then CRASH! BANG! WALLOP! The balloon landed right on top of James!

He was so scared, he let out a huge burst of steam. The balloon rose into the air again.

"Well done, James!" called his Driver.

"Your hot air did the trick!"

James and Thomas were not pleased.

"Oh no!" cried Thomas. "You saved it!"

The barrier lifted and Thomas puffed crossly away.

"I didn't mean to!" groaned James.

"Now it's bound to take our passengers."

When James arrived at the station,
The Fat Controller was waiting on the platform.
"Well done, James!" he said. "The balloon's pilot
told me that he was in trouble until you let out
your burst of steam."
"I wish I hadn't done it," said James. "Now the
passengers will ride in the balloon instead of
the train."

The Fat Controller laughed. "These holidaymakers are coming to ride in the balloon! But they will need a ride home – in a train!"

James was delighted. He whistled happily and went off to tell Thomas the good news.

The Fat Controller was right. The engines were busier than ever. They took holidaymakers to and from the airfield all day long. Thomas and Bertie sometimes raced each other to get passengers to the airfield first.

And that evening, as he rested after his busy day, Thomas dreamed that he could fly too . . .

Just like the red balloon!

First published in Great Britain 2002
by Egmont UK Limited
239 Kensington High Street, London W8 6SA
This edition published 2007

Thomas the Tank Engine & Friends™

A BRITT ALLCROFT COMPANY PRODUCTION

Based on The Railway Series by The Reverend W Awdry
© 2007 Gullane (Thomas) LLC. A HIT Entertainment Company

Thomas the Tank Engine & Friends and Thomas & Friends are trademarks of Gullane (Thomas) Limited.
Thomas the Tank Engine & Friends and Design is Reg. US. Pat. & Tm. Off.